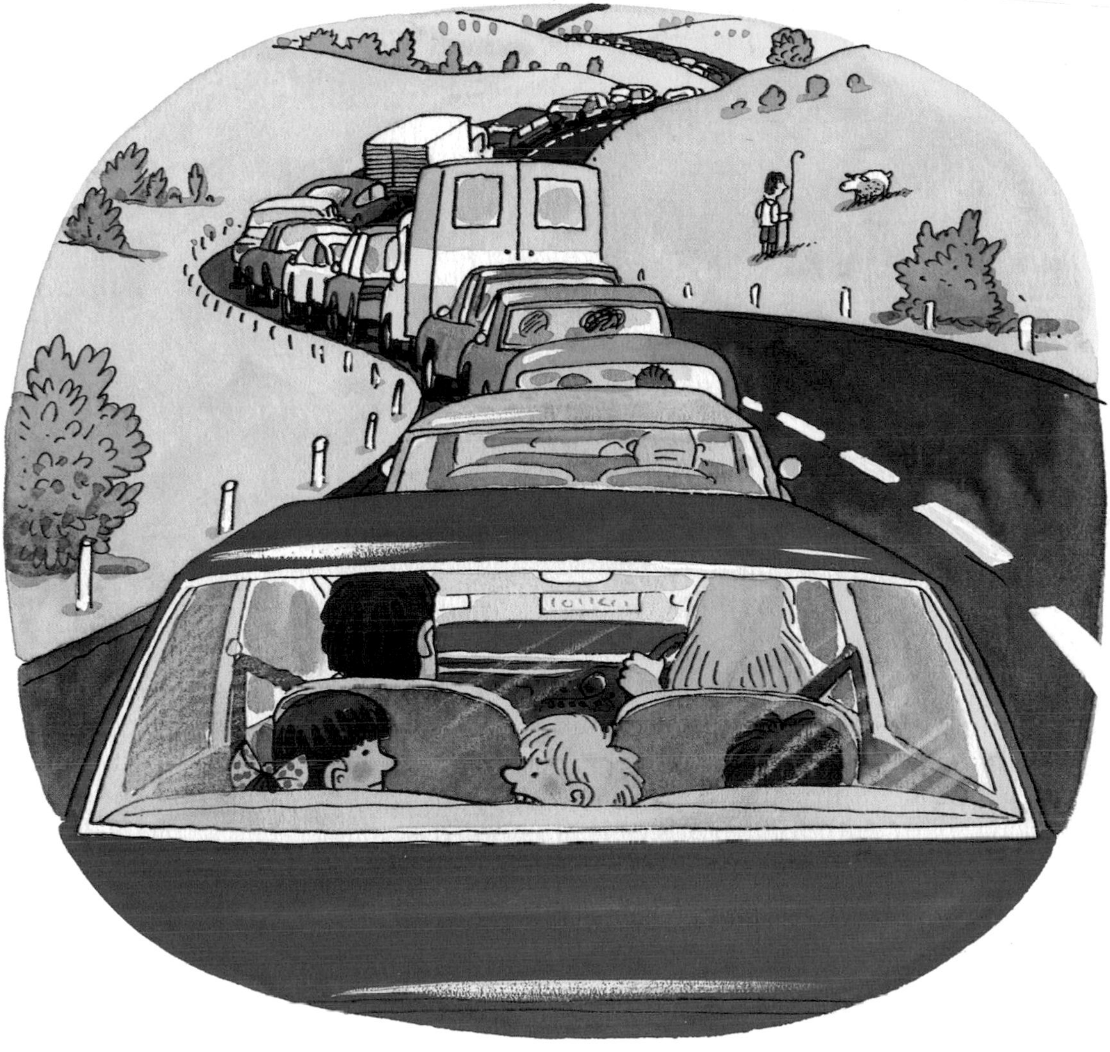

"I'm bored," said Kipper.

"I'm hungry," said Biff.

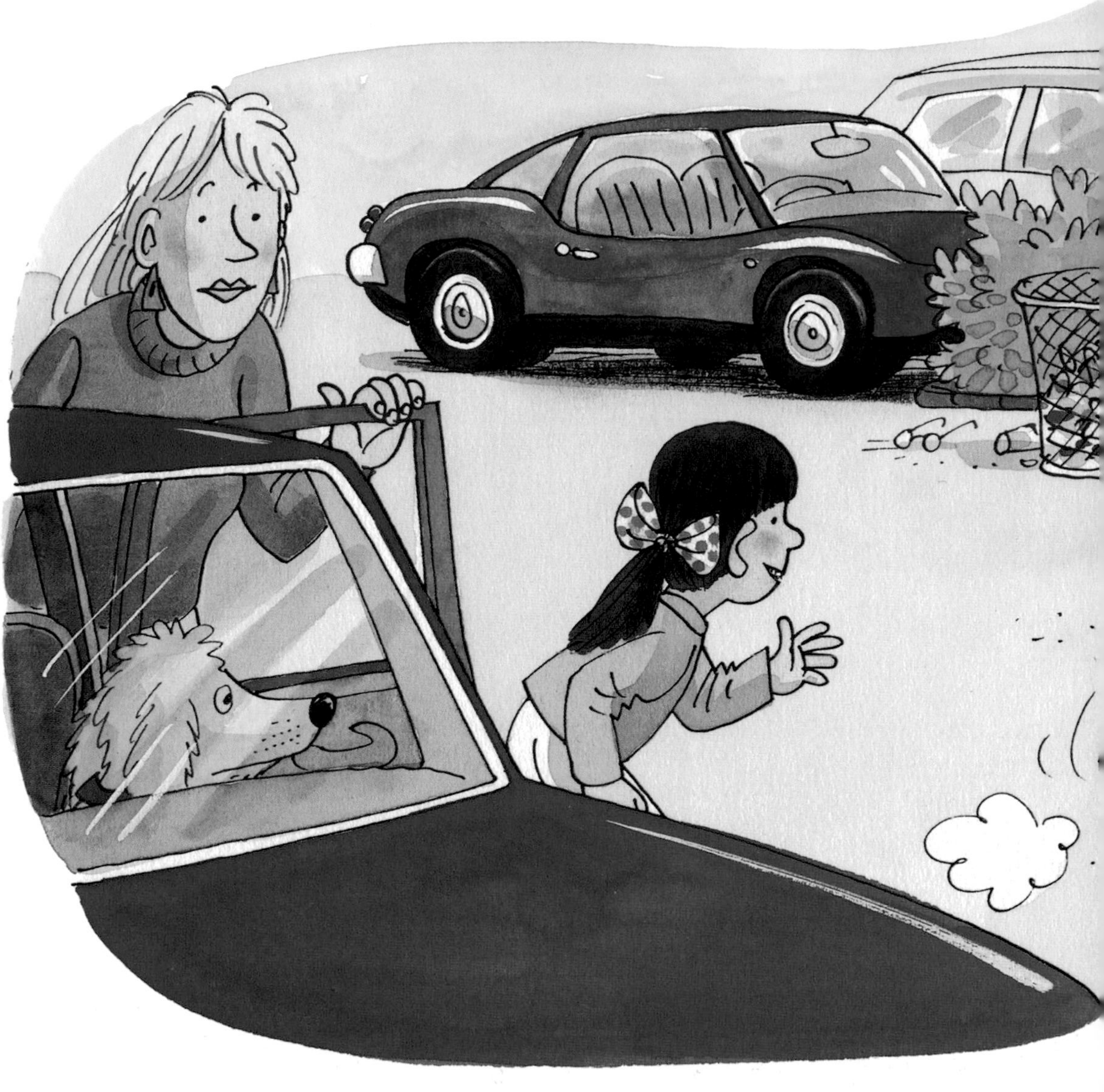

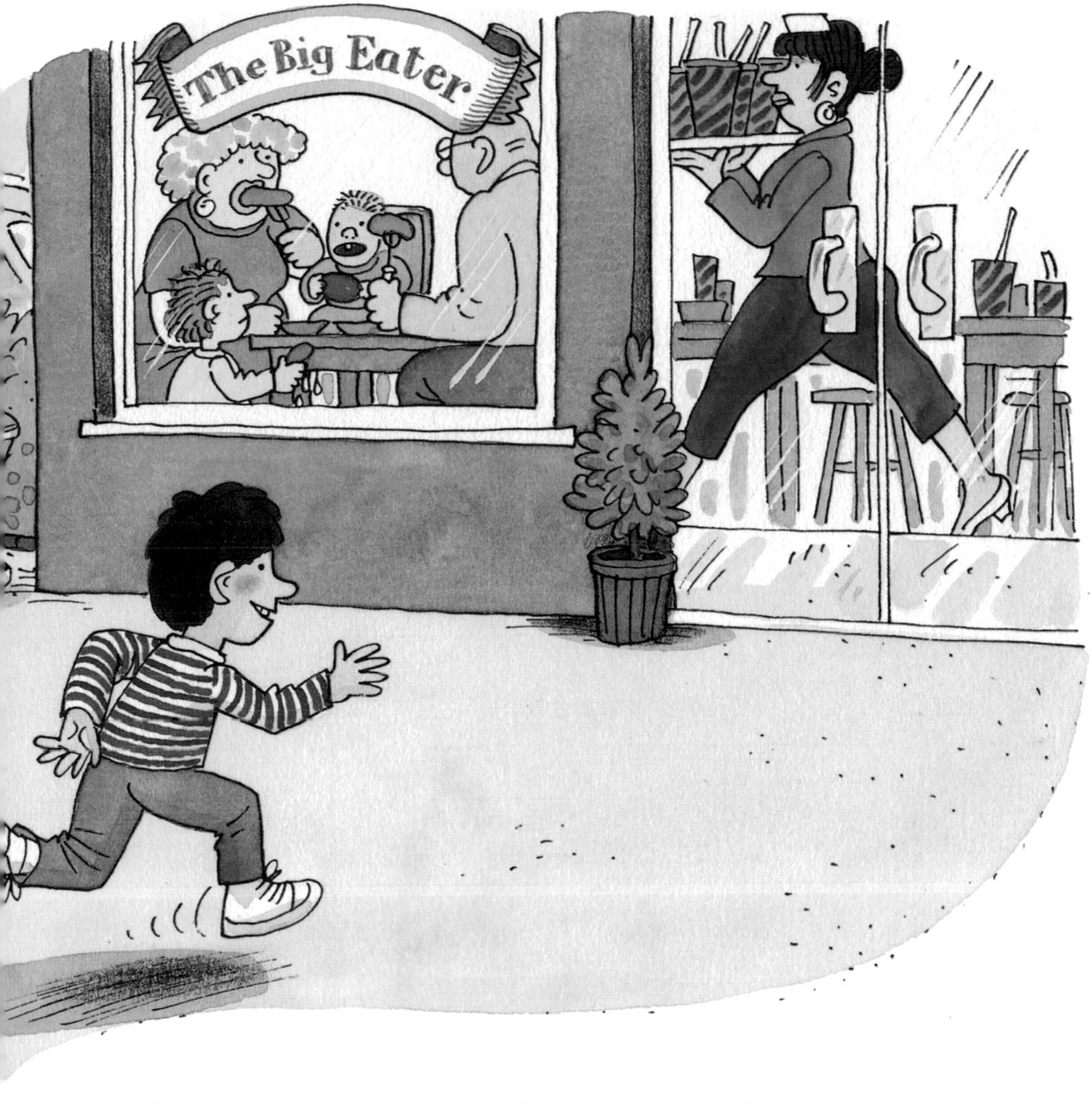

"I'm thirsty," said Chip.

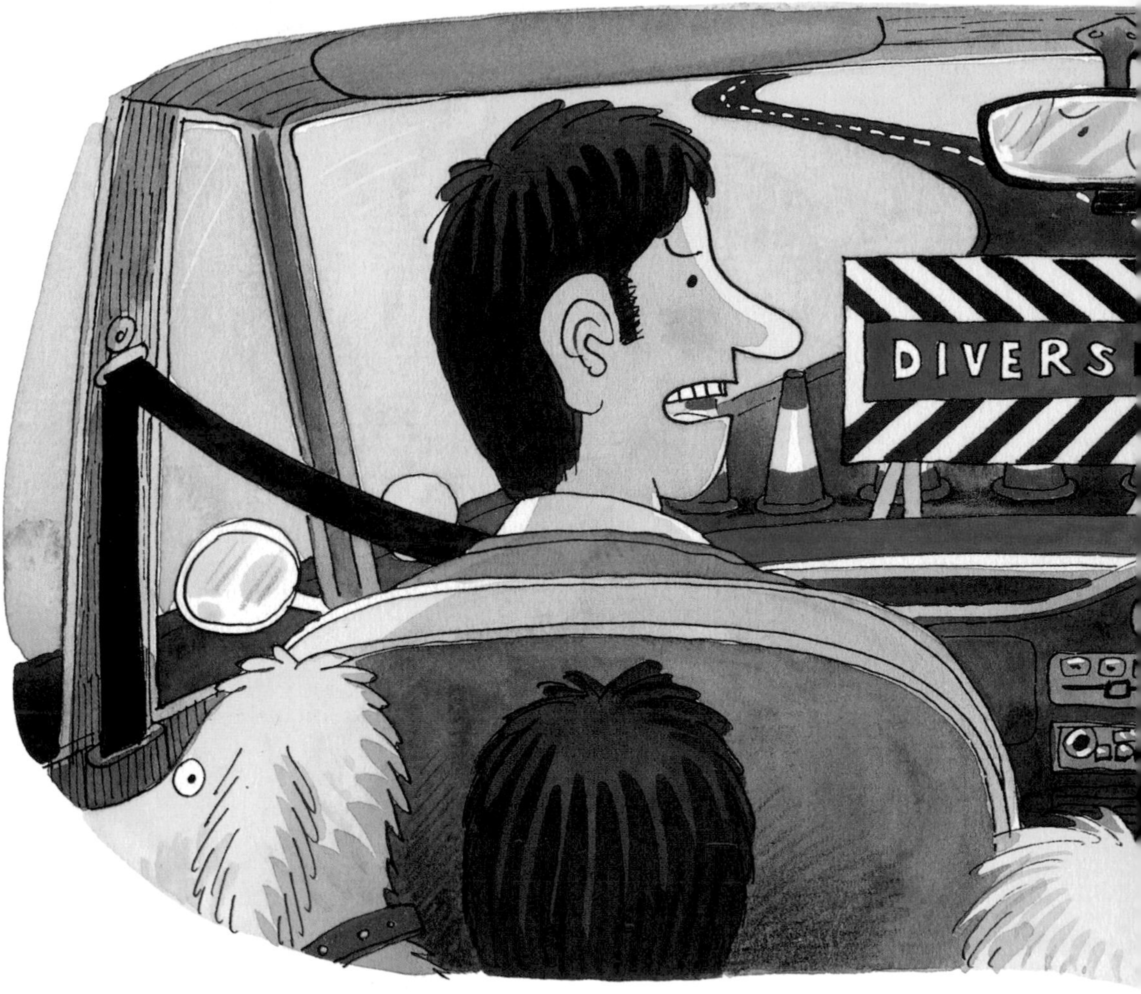

"I'm cross," said Dad.

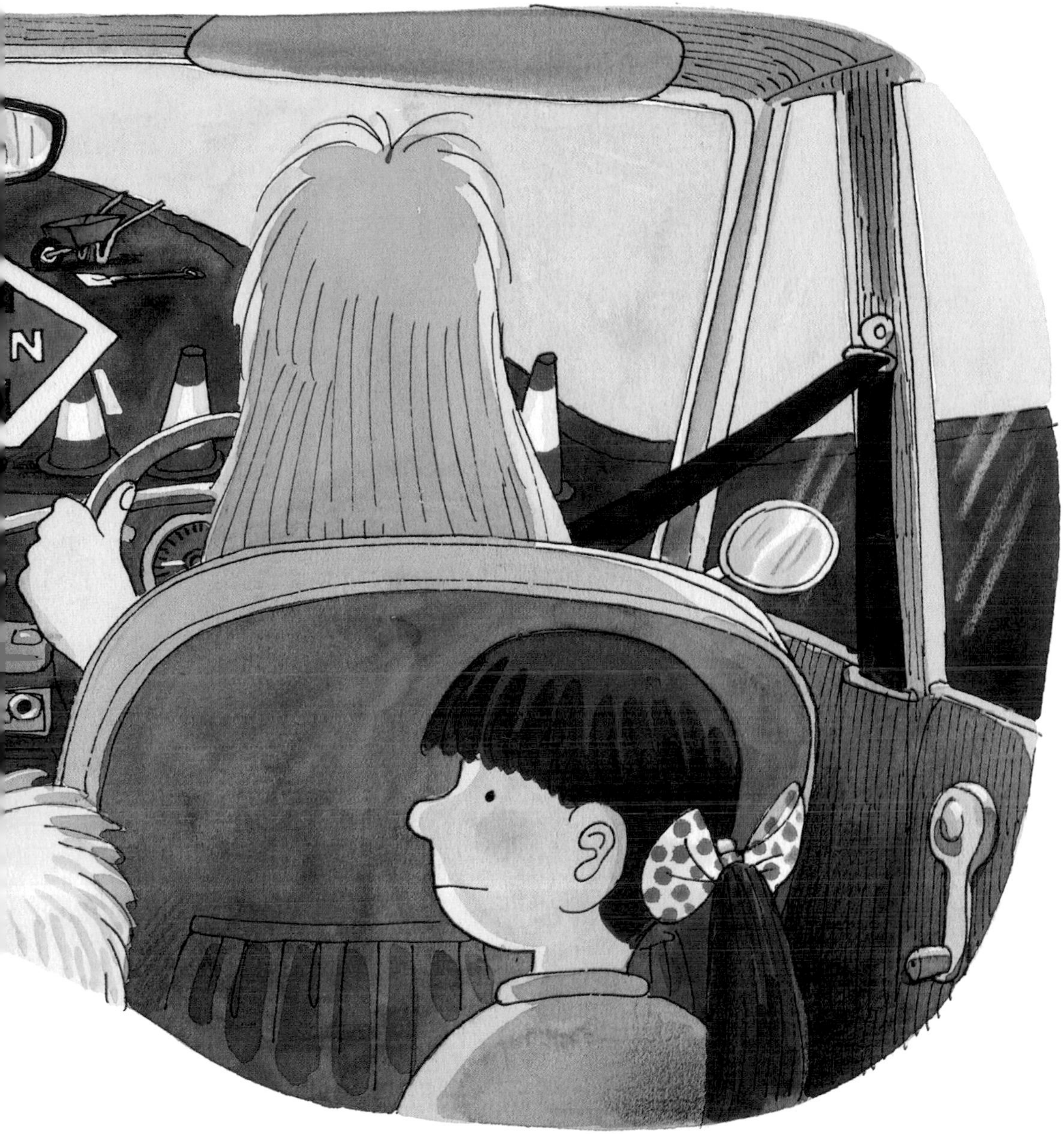

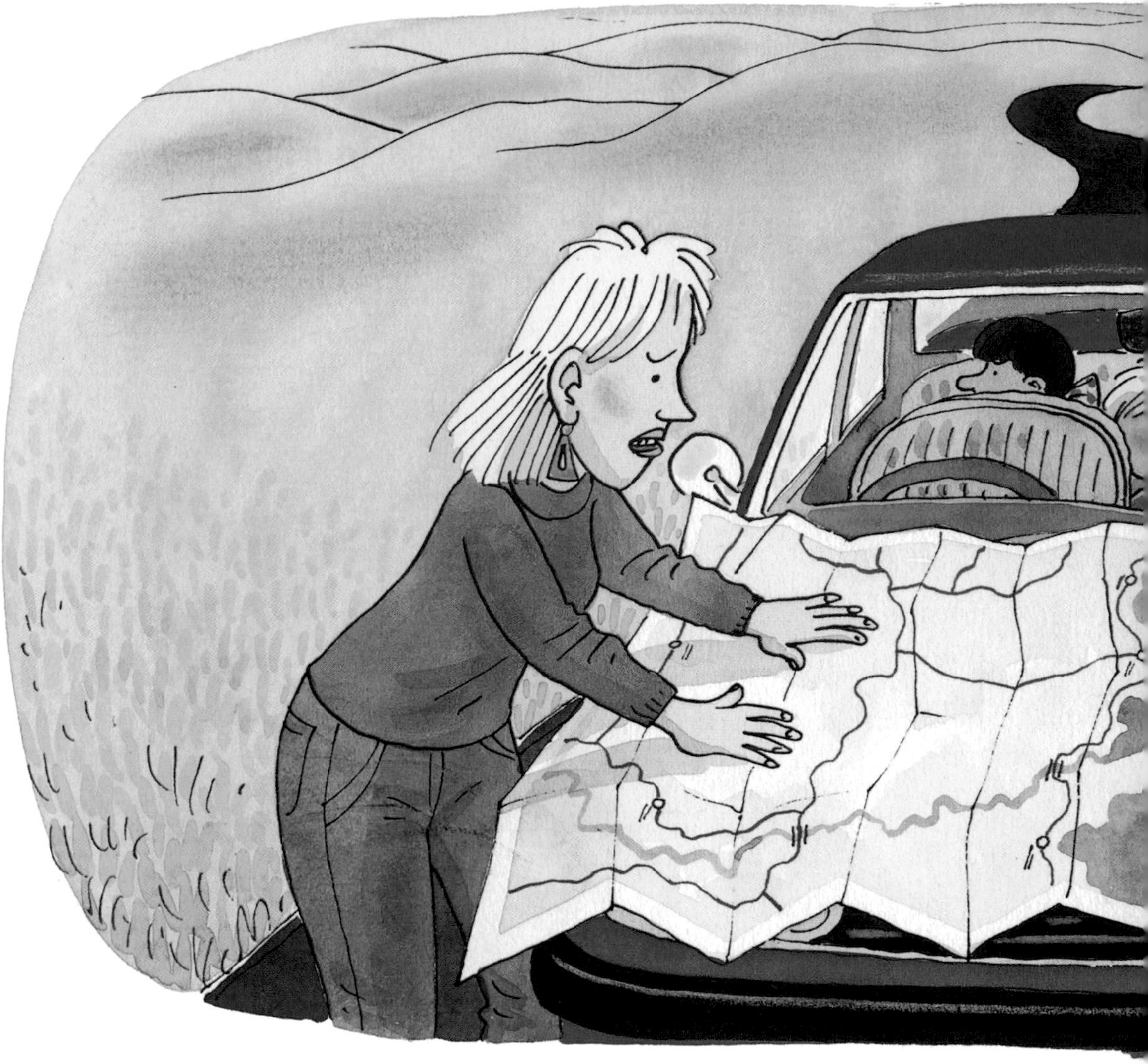

"I'm lost," said Mum.

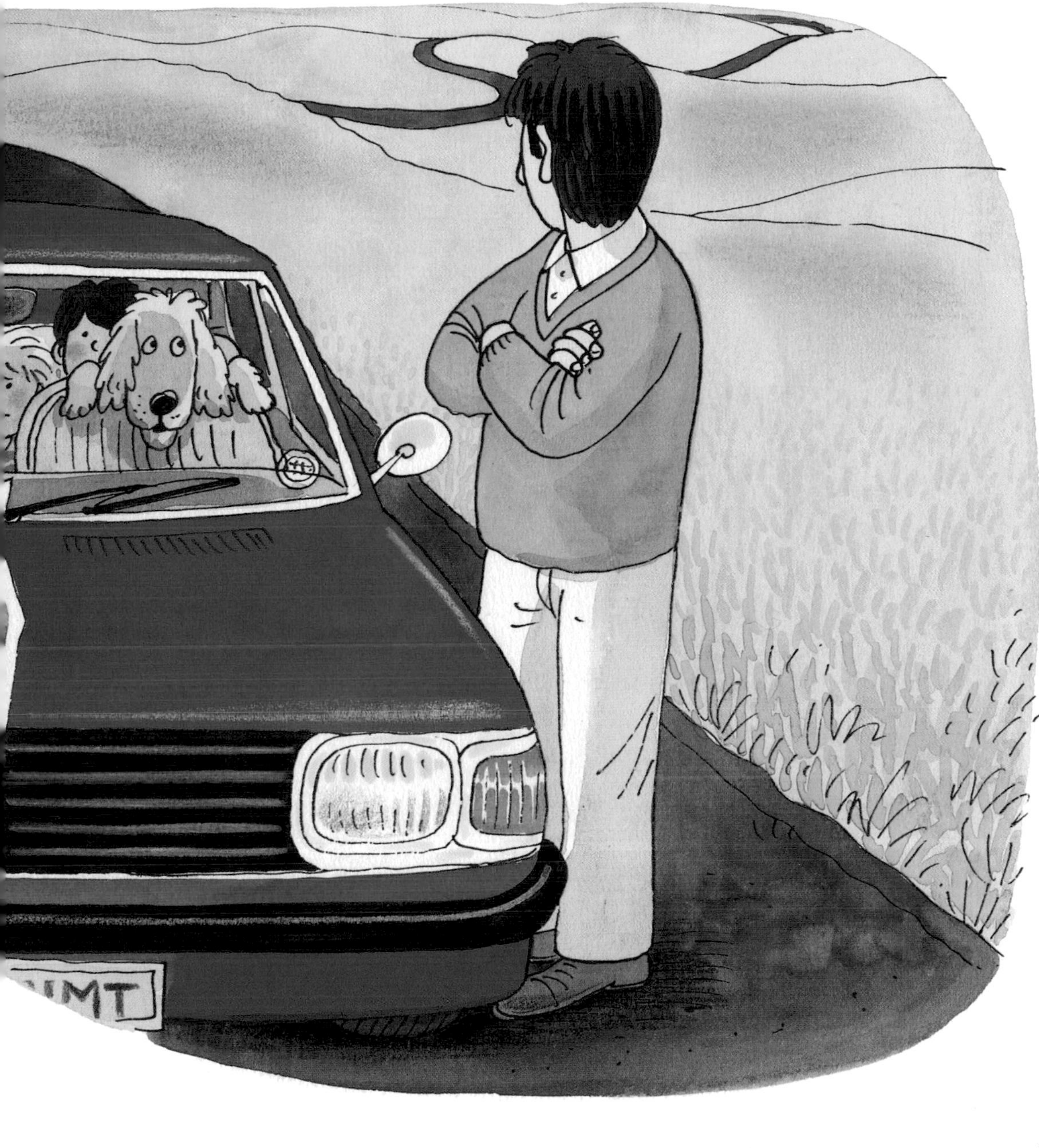
MT

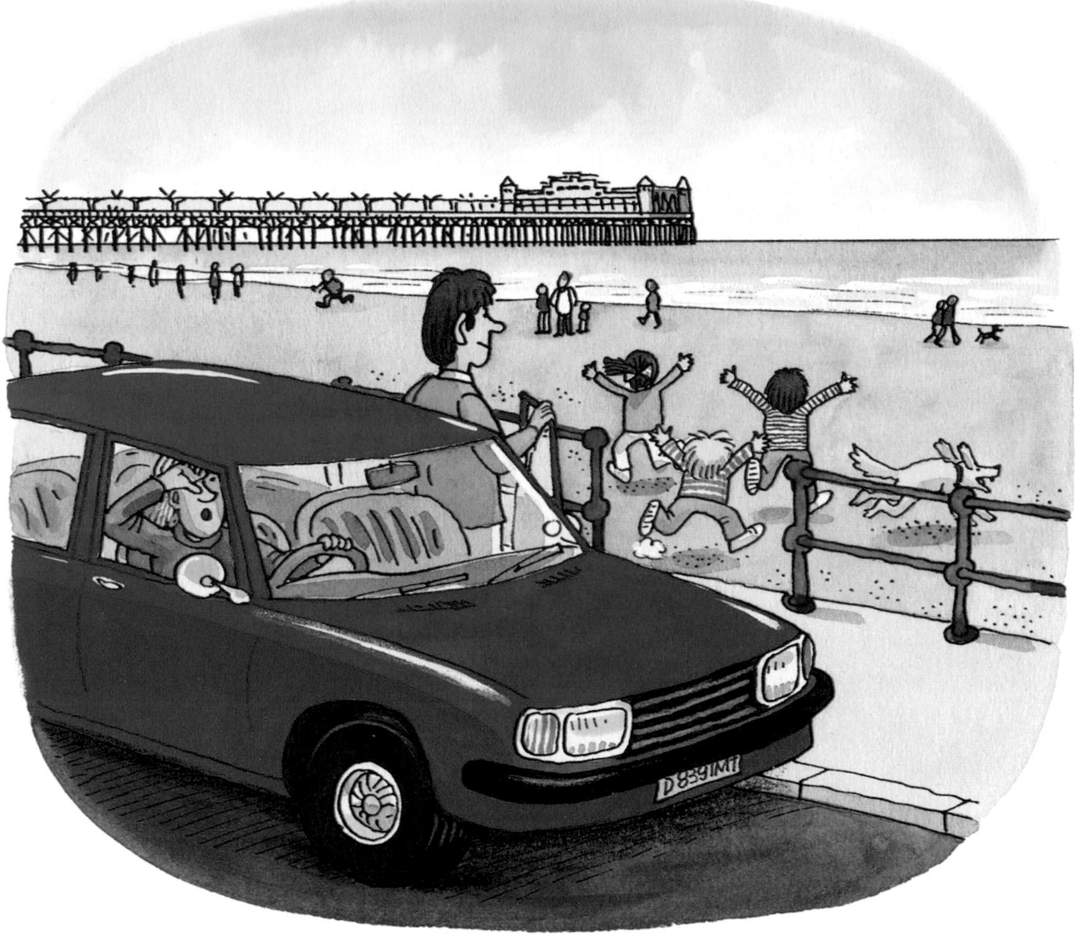

"Hooray!" said everyone.